AFRAID OF THE DARK?

By **Albin Sadar**

Illustrated by **Valerio Fabbretti**

Ready-to-Read

Simon Spotlight

New York London Toronto Sydney New Delhi

For all those who never had
a book dedicated to them—A. S.

To Mom and Dad—V. F.

SIMON SPOTLIGHT
An imprint of Simon & Schuster Children's Publishing Division
1230 Avenue of the Americas, New York, New York 10020
This Simon Spotlight edition October 2019
Text copyright © 2019 by Albin Sadar
Illustrations copyright © 2015, 2019 by Valerio Fabbretti
For information about special discounts for bulk purchases, please contact Simon & Schuster
Special Sales at 1-866-506-1949 or business@simonandschuster.com.
Manufactured in the United States of America 0819 LAK
10 9 8 7 6 5 4 3 2 1
This book has been cataloged with the Library of Congress.
ISBN 978-1-5344-2195-0 (hc)
ISBN 978-1-5344-2194-3 (pbk)
ISBN 978-1-5344-2196-7 (eBook)

Hamster Holmes and Dr. Watt
had just arrived at the
Fluffy Stay Inn.
They were excited to take a break
from detective work.

"Good evening,"
Hamster Holmes said to
the owner of the hotel,
a cat named Michelle Mouser.

"Welcome,"
Mrs. Mouser said.
"Let me show you to your room."
That was when Dr. Watt noticed
something strange.
At the end of the hallway,
the window curtains were moving.

Dr. Watt pointed and flashed a
message to Hamster Holmes.
Dr. Watt used Morse code to talk,
blinking his light on and off
to form dashes and dots.
A long flash of light was a dash.
A short flash of light was a dot.

"The curtains are moving?"
Hamster Holmes asked.
Dr. Watt nodded, and they went
to investigate.
He looked to see if the window
was open.
A gust of wind could have made
the curtains move.

"The window is shut tight,
so I do not think wind is to blame,"
Hamster Holmes said.
They did not see any other clues,
so they decided that this mystery
could wait until morning.

As Mrs. Mouser showed them to
their room, she told them,
"It is the second strange thing
to happen here since yesterday.
I am beginning to wonder if
my inn is haunted!"
Hamster Holmes and Dr. Watt
did not believe in ghosts,
but they asked her to explain.

"Last night, Corny O'Squirrel
was in his room. He thought he heard
the bell ring at the front desk,"
Mrs. Mouser told them,
"but when he looked out of his room,
no one was there!"
"That is strange,"
said Hamster Holmes,
and Dr. Watt agreed.

That night, the detectives
tried to forget about the
mysteries and enjoy their
vacation.
They played a game and tried
to relax.

Soon Hamster Holmes grew tired,
took a sip of milk, and went to bed.

Dr. Watt turned off the lights
and read a good mystery book by
candlelight.

Hamster Holmes was not usually
afraid of the dark, but when he saw
a shadow move, he sat up in bed.

Then he realized the shadow was coming from a tree branch and chuckled.

He quickly fell fast asleep and started snoring.

Suddenly, the sound of someone shouting "Yikes!" woke up everyone in the hotel.
Dr. Watt peeked out of the room. He followed the other guests to the front desk to find out what had happened.

It seemed like everyone had
a story to tell.
Alicia had seen a ball roll across
the floor all by itself.

Josiah had heard
something fall
and found his
book on the floor.

Ouchy had found
someone else's
hair in his favorite comb!

"I noticed something too,"
said Hamster Holmes,
joining the guests.
"The glass of milk on my night table
was full when I went to sleep,
but now it is almost empty!"

Hamster Holmes looked
down the hallway.
"Do any of you notice something
else that is odd?"
he asked the guests, but they
just shrugged.

"All the doors to the guest rooms
are open . . . except one!"
said Hamster Holmes.
"That room is not being used,"
said Mrs. Mouser,
"so that is why the door is closed.
The room is empty."

"Are you sure the room is empty?"
asked Hamster Holmes.
He went to the closed door
and knocked.
"Who is it?" someone asked from
inside the room.
Mrs. Mouser was shocked!
"I am Hamster Holmes.
May I come in?" he asked.

After a moment, the voice said, "Yes," and Hamster Holmes slowly opened the door.
At first, it seemed like no one was there.
Then Hamster Holmes noticed that the bed was very lumpy.

"Aha!" he said.
"The mystery is . . . solved!"
He pulled back the covers
and saw . . . three kittens!
"Hello and meow!" they said.

"Those are my nephews,
Fee, Fifo, and Fum!"
said Mrs. Mouser.
"They are supposed to be staying
in my room while their parents are
away. So what are you doing here?"
she asked the kittens.

The kittens looked ashamed.
"We didn't mean to
scare anyone," said Fee.
"We were just bored and wanted
to have fun," said Fifo.
Fum nodded.
Hamster Holmes explained,
"You were so small and fast
that no one ever saw you!"

The kittens promised to behave.
"We are sorry!" they said,
and Mrs. Mouser forgave them.
She was just happy that there were
no ghosts in her hotel!

Everyone slept well that night. The next day, they all joined the kittens in their favorite game: Yarnball!

Do you want to
solve mysteries like
Hamster Holmes and Dr. Watt?
Turn the page for a fun activity
and a special case to solve
with Morse code!

Solve the Mystery!

There is a new mystery to solve, and this time it is your turn to crack the code . . . and the case. When Russell the Woodpecker, Hamster Holmes, and Dr. Watt go to Corny O'Squirrel's house for a late-night snack of cookies and warm milk, a spoon goes missing. Corny looks everywhere, but he cannot find it.

Dr. Watt saw what happened, but he is having trouble getting the attention of his friends. Can you read the Morse code and help Dr. Watt tell his friends that he has solved the mystery?

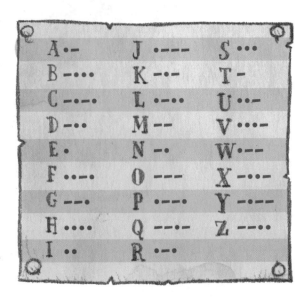

A •-	J •---	S •••
B -•••	K -•-	T -
C -•-•	L •-••	U ••-
D -••	M --	V •••-
E •	N -•	W •--
F ••-•	O ---	X -••-
G --•	P •--•	Y -•--
H ••••	Q --•-	Z --••
I ••	R •-•	

Check the answer key on the last page of this book when you are ready. You can also use the Morse code chart to write a secret message to a friend.

Find the Missing Words

Hamster Holmes loves books, reading, and everything about words. He also loves puzzles, but this one has him stumped. Can you help him find the words in this word jumble? Keep in mind that words can go from side to side or top to bottom.

CLOCK
FIREFLY
CLUE
EVIDENCE
HAMSTER

N	C	L	O	C	K
P	Z	E	J	N	R
F	R	V	T	E	H
I	U	I	L	R	A
R	A	D	K	H	M
E	B	E	Q	V	S
F	X	N	D	B	T
L	D	C	L	U	E
Y	L	E	A	Z	R

Great job, detective!

When you're done, you can check the answer key at the end of this book.

Do you want to be a detective like Hamster Holmes?

Here are some tips straight from the hamster himself:

What kinds of skills do detectives need?
You have to be someone who looks at the world around you for things that other people—or hamsters—don't notice. Clues can be found anywhere!

Do you have any tricks that help you solve mysteries?
I find that it helps to talk through the evidence aloud. Usually I talk to Dr. Watt, my partner in solving crimes. Sometimes I solve a mystery in the middle of a sentence!

What do you do when you feel stuck?
That's simple: I go for a run on the wheel. Exercise helps me come up with new ideas.

What advice do you have for anyone who wants to be a detective?
It is important to have a good partner—and it helps to find one who sees things a little differently from you. Dr. Watt sees the world from all different angles since he can fly, and he is a brilliant detective too. Without him I might not be able to say "This mystery is solved!" on every case!

Y	L	E	A	Z	R	
L	D	C	L	U	E	
F	X	N	D	B	T	
E	B	E	Q	V	S	
R	A	D	K	H	M	
I	U	I	L	R	A	
F	R	V	T	E	H	
P	N	E	J	N	R	
N	C	L	O	C	K	